PHOTOGRAPHY CREDITS: (c) ©Qilai Shen/Corbis Wire/Corbis; 3 (c) Thinkstock Images/
Jupiterimages/Getty Images; 7 (tr) ©Qilai Shen/Corbis Wire/Corbis

Printed in U.S.A.

ISBN: 978-0-544-07202-2

3 4 5 6 7 8 9 10 1083 21 20 19 18 17 16 15 14
4500470117   A B C D E F G

Magnets Help Us Every Day

by Kristen Kunkel

HOUGHTON MIFFLIN HARCOURT

Why do magnets stick to this steel door?

Magnets pull some objects to them. Magnets pull, or attract, objects made of iron or steel. These objects are magnetic.

Magnets help a doorbell work.

Magnets are in our homes. Magnets have different shapes and sizes.

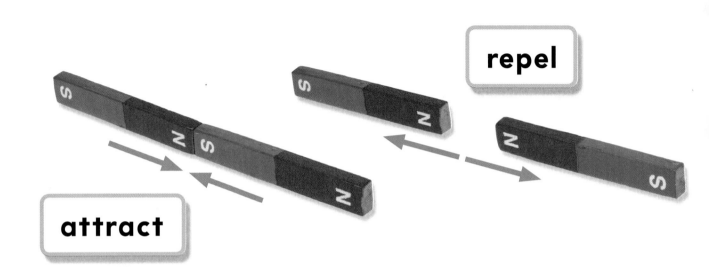

repel

attract

Magnets have two ends called poles.
Opposite poles attract. Same poles push
each other away, or repel.

Magnetic force pulls the toy car.

Magnets have a strong pull. They can attract iron or steel objects without touching them.

magnets at work

People use magnets at work. Some magnets are inside machines. Some magnets hold things together.

magnets on the train

magnets in the track

Magnets keep this train above the track.
Magnets help the train move very fast.

Explore Magnets

Draw a two-column chart on a piece of paper. Then choose six small objects. In the first column of the chart, list the objects you chose. Then test each object with a magnet to see if the magnet atracts it or not. In the second column, write "magnetic" or "not magnetic" for each object.

Write Sentences

Copy the following sentences on paper. Complete the sentences using the vocabulary words. Then write a sentence telling one way to use magnets at home.

1. Magnets _____ objects of iron or steel.

2. Something a magnet attracts is _____.

3. On magnets, like poles attract. Opposite poles _____.

Vocabulary

attract	poles
magnetic	repel
magnets	